Lincolnshire
COUNTY COUNCIL

COMMUNITIES, CULTURAL SERVICES
and ADULT EDUCATION
**This book should be returned on or before
the last date shown below.**

MEIA

To renew or order library books please telephone 01522 782010
or visit www.lincolnshire.gov.uk
You will require a Personal Identification Number.
Ask any member of staff for this.

199 (LIBS): RS/L5/19

D1350687

First Flight

04516872

Titles in First Flight

Badger Publishing Limited
15 Wedgwood Gate, Pin Green Industrial Estate,
Stevenage, Hertfordshire SG1 4SU
Telephone: 01438 356907. Fax: 01438 747015
www.badger-publishing.co.uk
enquiries@badger-publishing.co.uk

Shhh! My Family Are Spies ISBN 1 84424 837 2

Series Editor: Jonny Zucker
Publisher: David Jamieson
Commissioning Editor: Carrie Lewis
Editor: Paul Martin
Design: Fiona Grant
Illustration: Bob Doucet

SHHH! MY FAMILY ARE SPIES

Jane Langford

Contents

The secret meeting

Tom's new Nan was a spy. He had seen the proof with his own eyes.

She had papers in her handbag. They were yellow papers with black words. Tom had seen the words PLATO PLAN at the top of them.

Nan picked up her handbag. She pushed the yellow papers in and shut the bag.

"I'm going out!" she shouted. Then the door went BANG!

Tom had to act fast. He had to know what the papers were.

"Mum! Can I take the dog for a walk?" he yelled.

"Yes, but don't be long," said Mum.

Tom had only been with his new family for a year. Did Mum and Dad know that Nan was a spy? He didn't think so.

Tom and Scamp left the house.
They followed Nan down the street.

She went into a dark alley.

Tom was scared. What was Nan
doing here?

Two cats in the alley saw Scamp.
They hissed at him.

Nan jumped. She looked back.

Tom hid behind a big bin.
Wow! It smelt. But Nan hadn't seen
him. She went on up the alley. Then
went up some steps.

Tom and Scamp ran up the alley.
They hid by the steps.

Tom could hear Nan talking to a man.

"Ah!" said the man, "The Plato Plan!"

"Yes," said Nan.

"It's time we talked about money," said the man.

Money! His Nan must be selling secret plans. Most Nans don't sell secret plans!

Why did his new Nan have to be different?

Who or what is PLATO?

The next day Tom wanted to go to the library.

"Do you want to get a book out?" Mum said.

"No," said Tom, "I just want to look something up."

Tom went to the lady at the desk. "Have you got any books about Plato?" he asked.

The library lady put on her glasses. "Plato?" she asked. "Come over here."

Tom followed her.

"Look in this book," she said.

Tom took the book. It was very, very big.

He looked at the first page. There was nothing about Plato here.

He turned over. Still nothing.

"Can I help?" asked the library lady. "What word are you looking for?"

"Plato," said Tom.

"Then you need to find the words that start with P," said the library lady.

Of course! Tom soon found Plato. Plato was a very clever man. But he was dead! And he was not a spy.

"What are you looking at?"
asked Mum.

Tom jumped. Then Mum looked at the
book and she jumped too. "Er –
Plato," she said. "That's a funny thing
to be looking up."

Oh no! His new mum knew about
the PLATO PLAN! Maybe she was
a spy too.

My nan's a spy

Tom did not sleep all night.
His new family was very kind.
He was so happy with them.
Well… he had been.

But now? Tom did not know what
to think.

Three weeks ago the phone had rung
very late at night.
Nan had picked it up.
From then on, things had been odd.
Nan kept going out.
Then there were the yellow plans and
the trip down the alley.
What was going on…?

The next morning he was very pale.
His eyes were big and black.

"What's wrong?" asked Mum.

"I got no sleep," said Tom.

"Oh dear!" said Mum. "No school for you today. Go back to bed and get some sleep."

Tom did as he was told.

When the house was quiet, he got out of bed and went to the top of the stairs. Mum and Dad were talking very, very quietly in the kitchen.

"Do you think he knows?" asked Dad.

"Yes," said Mum. "He followed Nan out of the house. Then he looked up Plato in the library!"

Dad shook his head. "This is not what we wanted!"

"No!" said Mum. "It isn't!"

Tom was shocked. Dad was in on it too.

Tom ran back to his bedroom. Nan was a spy and Mum and Dad knew all about it.

A cunning plan

The next day Tom took Scamp for a long walk. He needed to think.

What should he do?
He walked and walked and walked.

"I need more proof," said Tom at last.
"I can't just say, 'My Nan is a spy'."

Tom knew what he must do. He must find Nan's bag. The yellow plans with the black words were in there. They were proof!

Tom worked out a plan. He had to wait until the house was quiet.

He waited in his bedroom until Dad went to work. Mum went to the shops, then Nan sat down by the TV.

The time had come!

Tom crept into his Nan's bedroom.
He was very scared.

The handbag was not on the bed.

Tom looked under the bed. Nothing there.

He looked under the chair.
Nothing there.

Then, suddenly, he saw it. It was on top of the wardrobe.

Tom stood on the bed and pulled it down.

THUMP!
It landed on the floor!
Tom held his breath.
Had Nan heard?

All was quiet. All was still.
Tom did not move.

Nothing. No sound. No movement.

At last, Tom put his hand into the bag.
The yellow papers must be there. Yes!

He took them out.

But it wasn't the plans.
It was money!
A big pile of money!

The door opened. Nan came in.
She saw Tom with her money.

"TOM!" she shouted.

Tom fell back, terrified.

"Er – Nan!" he said in shock.

Nan's eyes filled with tears. She shook her head. "If you want some pocket money, Tom, you just have to ask."

"I don't want your money!" shouted Tom. "I just wanted proof that you're a spy."

"A SPY?" said Nan.

"Yes!" shouted Tom, "I know all about the PLATO PLAN! You were selling secret plans. I saw them!"

"What?" said Nan.

Tom held up the money.

"And this is the money you got for selling the plans!"

The secret is out

Nan did not know what to say.
She sat on the bed. She looked as if
she was going to cry. But then she
laughed and laughed and laughed.

"Oh Tom!" she said. "I did have some
secret plans. But I did not sell them.
I have got to pay for them!"

"Pay for them?" said Tom,
"What do you mean?"

Nan got up off the bed and smiled.
"Come with me," she said.

Tom was scared. What was going on?

"Come on," she said again.

"OK," he said.

Nan led Tom out of the house. She took him into the dark alley.

"This is where you came before!" said Tom.

Nan led Tom up the steps and took him into a room full of red and green lights.

Balloons hung from a net.
A long table was full of food.
It was a party room!

"What's this?" said Tom.

"This," smiled Nan, "is the PLATO PLAN."

She took the yellow plans out of her pocket.

"Look at the door. PLATO is the name of this club. The money is to pay for a party at this club!"

"A party?" said Tom. "But who is having a party?" he asked.

"You are!" shouted Mum and Dad.

Tom gasped. "Me?"

"Yes. It's a party for you, Tom," said Dad. "We are going to be your real Mum and Dad at last."

"My real Mum and Dad?" said Tom. "But how? I thought we had to wait."

"We did! But now it's all fixed!" said Mum. "From today, you belong to us. Are you happy?"

Happy?

Tom looked at Nan. "You're not a spy?"

"No."

He turned to his Mum and Dad.

"Nor you?"

They shook their heads.

"No."

Then Tom smiled.

"I'm happy!" he said.

"HOORAY!" yelled everyone.

Tom's ears rang with cheers.

All his friends jumped out at him.
Mum and Dad threw balloons into the
air.

"THREE CHEERS FOR THE PLATO
PLAN!"